CLIMBING JACOB'S LADDER

CLIMBING JACOB'S LADDER

Heroes of the Bible in African-American Spirituals

Selected and edited by John Langstaff
Illustrated by Ashley Bryan
Piano arrangements by John Andrew Ross

MARGARET K. McELDERRY BOOKS
New York

Maxwell Macmillan Canada
Toronto

Maxwell Macmillan International
New York   Oxford   Singapore   Sydney

For Peter and Rebecca
—J.L.

To the memory of my friends:
William Wallace and Lydia Weber
"One more river to cross"
—A.B.

Margaret K. McElderry Books
Macmillan Publishing Company
866 Third Avenue
New York, NY 10022

Maxwell Macmillan Canada, Inc.
1200 Eglinton Avenue East
Suite 200
Don Mills, Ontario M3C 3N1

First edition
Printed in Hong Kong
10 9 8 7 6 5 4 3 2 1

Library of Congress Cataloging-in-Publication Data
Climbing Jacob's ladder : heroes of the Bible in African-American
spirituals / selected and edited by John Langstaff ; illustrated by
Ashley Bryan ; piano arrangements by John Andrew
Ross. — 1st ed.
9 scores.
For piano.
Includes chord symbols.
Summary: An illustrated collection of black spirituals about Old
Testament heroes.
ISBN 0-689-50494-2
1. Spirituals (Songs)—Juvenile. [1. Spirituals (Songs)]
I. Langstaff, John M.   II. Bryan, Ashley, ill.   III. Ross, John
Andrew.
M1670.C65   1991   90-27297

The original pictures for *Climbing Jacob's Ladder: Heroes of*
the Bible in African-American Spirituals are tempera paintings.

When God found that Noah and his family were the only good people left on Earth, he decided to destroy everyone else in a great flood. God showed Noah how to build an ark big enough to hold his family and a pair of each kind of animal in the world. Then God sent torrents of rain lasting forty days and nights. After that, Noah sent out a bird that found dry land, and God put the rainbow in the sky.

Didn't It Rain?

Abraham, a descendant of Noah, was a good man. God wanted him to have many children because those children would become great leaders of the ancient world. Abraham loved his children dearly. Abraham saw all his family grow up around him, since he lived to be a very, very old man.

Rock-a My Soul

Begin softly; repeat ad lib, growing louder

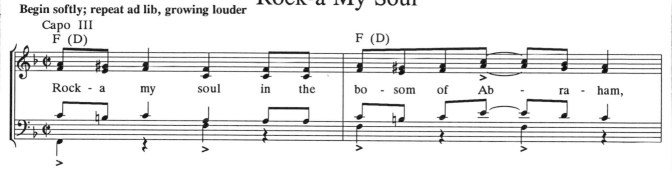

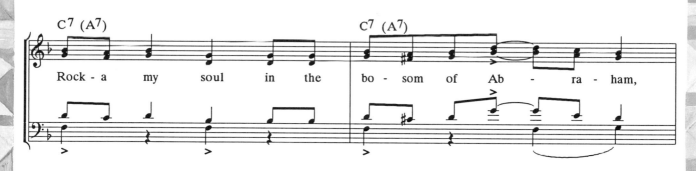

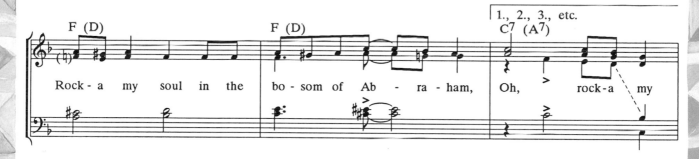

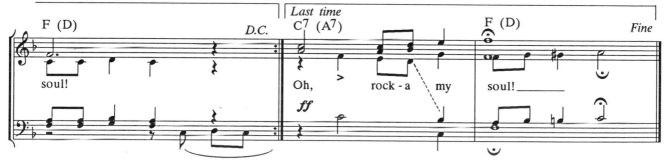

Note: This is often sung with a strong dotted feeling throughout (♪♩ ♩ ♪).

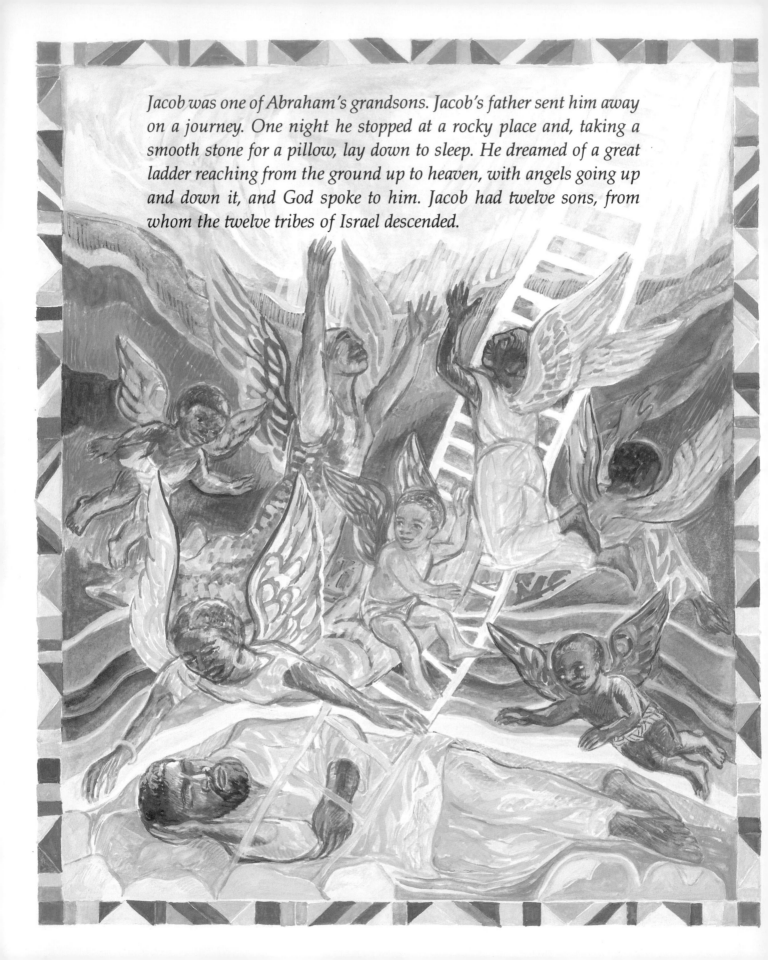

Jacob was one of Abraham's grandsons. Jacob's father sent him away on a journey. One night he stopped at a rocky place and, taking a smooth stone for a pillow, lay down to sleep. He dreamed of a great ladder reaching from the ground up to heaven, with angels going up and down it, and God spoke to him. Jacob had twelve sons, from whom the twelve tribes of Israel descended.

We Are Climbing Jacob's Ladder

With a steady, firm gospel beat

We are climb - ing Ja - cob's lad - der,
Ev' - ry rung goes high - er, high - er,

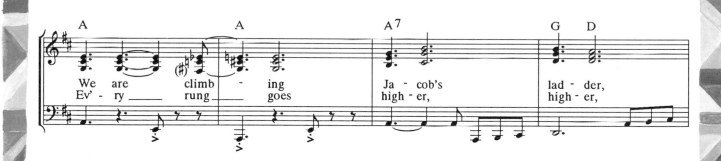

We are climb - ing Ja - cob's lad - der,
Ev' - ry rung goes high - er, high - er,

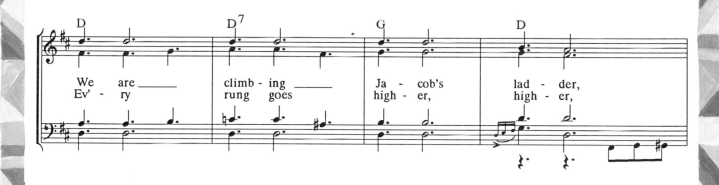

We are climb - ing Ja - cob's lad - der,
Ev' - ry rung goes high - er, high - er,

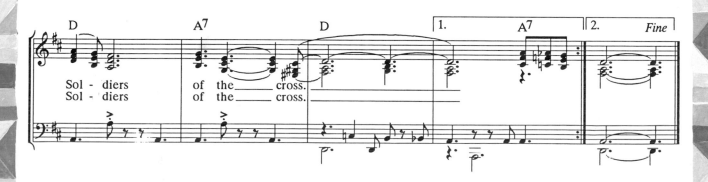

Sol - diers of the cross.
Sol - diers of the cross.

Fine

Moses was one of the greatest leaders of the ancient world. His people, the Israelites, were slaves under the Pharaoh, the harsh ruler of Egypt. God caused strange and terrible things to happen to the Pharaoh, so that finally he agreed to let Moses lead the people of Israel out of Egypt on a long, long walk, to a land of their own.

Go Down, Moses

Slow, with a flowing rubato

When   Is - rael was in   E - gypt land,   "Let my   peo - ple   go."   Op -
"Thus   saith the Lord," bold   Mo - ses   said.   "Let my   peo - ple   go.   If

pressed so   hard they   could not   stand,   "Let my   peo - ple   go."
not, I'll   strike your   first born   dead!   Let my   peo - ple   go."

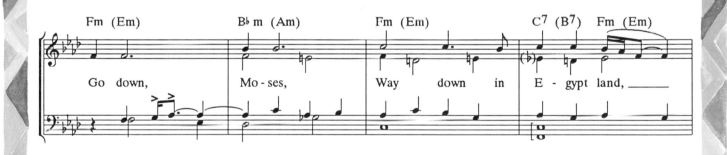

Go down,   Mo - ses,   Way   down   in   E - gypt land, _____

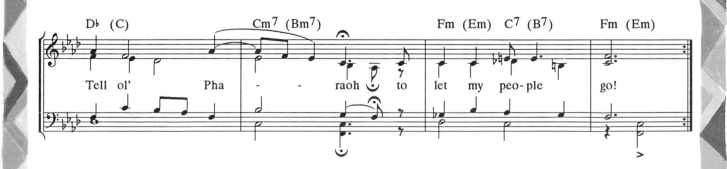

Tell ol'   Pha - - raoh   to   let my peo - ple   go!

When Moses died, Joshua became the leader of the Israelites. On their way to the Promised Land, they had to capture the city of Jericho. They circled the city each day, led by priests blowing rams' horns. On the last day, as the trumpets sounded, Joshua commanded his army to give a great shout, and the walls of the city tumbled down.

Joshua Fit the Battle of Jericho

Rhythmic; lively, but not too fast

Capo III

The shepherd boy David was a musician who played the harp and sang for the king. One day he saved the king's army by killing the giant, Goliath, with his slingshot. He later became the king of Israel.

Little David, Play on Your Harp

Rhythmic

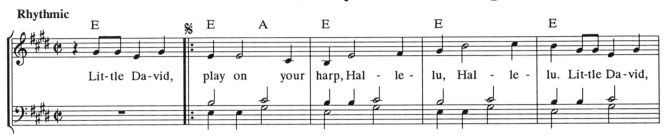

Lit-tle Da-vid, play on your harp, Hal - le - lu, Hal - le - lu. Lit-tle Da-vid,

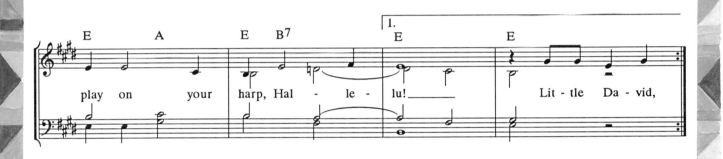

play on your harp, Hal - le - lu! ___ Lit - tle Da - vid,

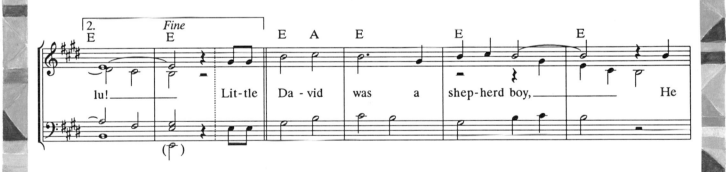

2. *Fine*

lu! ___ Lit-tle Da - vid was a shep-herd boy,___ He

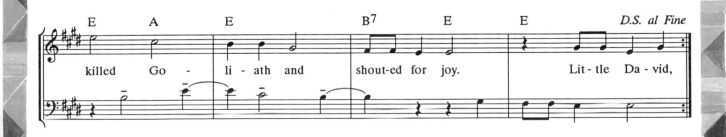

D.S. al Fine

killed Go - li - ath and shout-ed for joy. Lit - tle Da - vid,

Ezekiel was a religious teacher in the Near East. Like many prophets, he saw powerful and extraordinary visions, which he described as coming from God. They helped him in his teaching. Bright, fiery wheels turning in the sky was one of those visions.

Ezekiel Saw the Wheel

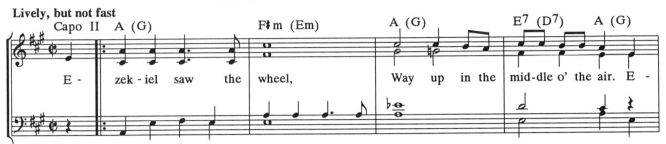

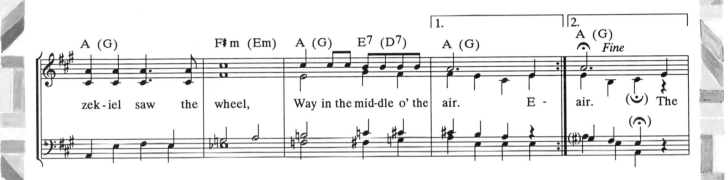

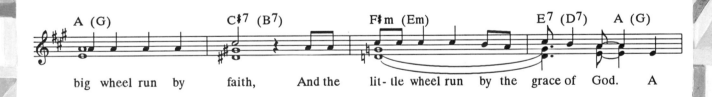

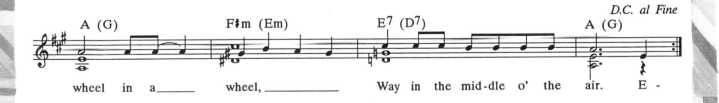

Young Daniel, because of his religious beliefs, was thrown into a deep pit filled with lions that would kill him. The next morning, brave Daniel was still alive. God had saved him from the fierce lions.

Didn't My Lord Deliver Daniel?

Jonah disobeyed God and then fled in fear on a ship. God created a fierce storm, and the sailors, blaming Jonah for bringing bad luck to them, threw him overboard and he was swallowed by a giant whale. In the belly of the whale, Jonah prayed to God for forgiveness. God, hearing Jonah, had the whale spew him up on dry land.

Wake Up! Jonah

Note to teachers, parents, and instrumentalists

From among the many beautiful African-American spirituals, we have chosen those concerning the great prophets and legendary heroes of the Bible. People of all ages are drawn to the strong melodies and rhythms of these songs. Young children can make up additional verses of their own to sing, once they are familiar with the stories. Parents and teachers are encouraged to read and tell to children those extraordinary biblical tales as background to these spirituals.

Only in a few instances are there examples of Black English words in this collection. They are fitting and traditional; in fact, the dropping of certain consonants, while singing these songs, gives a more natural flow to the enunciation. Aspects of the music go back to African musical tradition, as well as to revival-meeting hymns and slave songs of the 1800s. Beneath the words of these spirituals lie other meanings—of bondage, hope, and freedom. All of these strands have been woven together into a powerful and meaningful form of song—an outpouring of personal faith and a people's creative music-making unmatched in the history of American music.

The suggested harmonies for guitar chords do not necessarily follow the chords of the piano accompaniment, for the two instrumentalists would probably not play together. As with most traditional music, spirituals can be sung effectively with no accompaniment. For less experienced guitarists, we have indicated alternative chord shapes to use with a capo: Attach the capo on the first, second, or third fret as noted, and then play the chords in parenthesis.